PLEASING THE BOSS

A FIRST TIME LESBIAN SPANKING

JOSIE BALE

PLEASING THE BOSS

© 2023 by Josie Bale

Cover by Reba Bale

CONTENTS

1. About This Book   1

2. Stay in Touch with Josie Bale   3

3. Chapter One: Getting Caught   4

4. Chapter Two: Getting More Than I Bar-   13
    gained For

5. Chapter Three: Not the Hairbrush!   22

6. Chapter Four: Riding My Face   31

7. Special Preview: The Reluctant Bride's First   38
    Spanking by Josie Bale

8. Other Books by Josie Bale   45

9. About Josie Bale   48

ABOUT THIS BOOK

Eavesdropping on a spanking leads to one of her own!

When Brandy overhears one of her coworkers getting **punished** at the office she's intrigued. Maybe a little turned on. She can't help but **fantasize** about her boss Sasha using her famously stern demeanor to redden her behind – and more.

When Sasha catches her spying instead of working, the naughty assistant gets a taste of what it's like to be **spanked by the boss**. Sasha has a firm hand – and a hard hairbrush – ready to do the job.

Brandy never expected that being punished would **hurt so good**. Or that a spanking could be so arousing. She's not the only one excited though...

Brandy's next assignment will involve pleasuring her **dominant** boss until she's completely **satisfied**!

"Pleasing the Boss" is part of the Sapphic Submission series. These sexy and fun stories follow the adventures of the employees at WLW Technology, where getting in trouble can lead to bare bottomed punishments from the lesbians in charge. These books are intended for mature audiences.

Be sure to check out a free preview of book one of the Spanking Therapy Clinic series, "The Reluctant Bride's First Spanking" at the end of this book!

STAY IN TOUCH WITH JOSIE BALE

You can stay up to date on all of Josie Bale's sexy spanking stories by following her at https://www. amazon.com/author/josiebale. You'll receive an email notifying you of all new releases!

CHAPTER ONE: GETTING CAUGHT

"**A**lina, you've been a very naughty girl!"

My face flushed as I heard the distinctive sound of something striking my coworker's ass. A paddle maybe or perhaps a belt.

Thwack!

Alina moaned, but I couldn't tell whether it was in pleasure or from the pain of the spanking she was receiving from her boss. I pressed my ear more firmly against the wood of the door, eager to hear everything.

Thwack!

Thwack!

My panties dampened as I continued to eavesdrop. I knew it was wrong, but I couldn't pull myself away.

I closed my eyes, imagining myself in the same position with my own boss, Sasha. Would Sasha drape me over her desk? Or maybe take me over her knees? I pressed my thighs together tight, trying to lessen the ache as fantasy and reality merged.

I wasn't sure what was wrong with me. I wasn't normally nosy, but when I happened to walk by the office of Ruth Jacobs, one of the executives here at WLW Technology, and heard some unusual sounds, I'd been compelled to stop and listen. I'd heard that some of the bosses at our lesbian-owned firm were into BDSM – allegedly someone in accounting had seen several of them at some underground sex dungeon -- but I'd chalked it all up to rumors.

Until tonight.

The only thing that surprised me more than learning that the BDSM rumors were true was that people were doing it at the office. And it wasn't late either, only just after five o'clock. There were still lots of people in the office. Acting out people's spanking fantasies at work didn't seem very professional. Then again, the way it made me feel wasn't very professional either.

"Brandy! What are you doing there?"

I nearly jumped out of my skin at the sound of Sasha's stern voice behind me. Crap. My boss had just busted me eavesdropping on someone's spanking like a nosy teenager. I straightened my spine and turned around slowly, trying to compose myself. Maybe I could just play this off as something else?

"Oh. Hey, Sasha. I was just, um, looking for Alina."

Thwack!

"Ahhh!"

We both looked towards the door as a loud moan pierced the air following the sound of something making an impact on skin. Again.

"It sounds like she and Ruth are otherwise engaged," Sasha said wryly.

I noticed that she didn't seem at all surprised – or flustered -- by the sounds coming from her colleague's office.

Another smack sounded, followed by a gasp. Of pain or pleasure, I couldn't say. My clit started throbbing in response.

"I had no idea you were such a Peeping Tom," Sasha said, tilting her head towards the door. Her voice was cold as ice. "One might think you have better things to do, like work on the Cross project."

My face flushed in embarrassment as I struggled to find an excuse – any excuse – for my behavior, but I came up empty. I needed to just suck it up and take responsibility for my actions.

"I'm...I'm sorry Sasha, this was clearly inappropriate. I'll just head back to my office and get back to work," I said in a small voice.

"No, you will come with me," she corrected. "I want to see you in my office. Now."

Sasha turned on her heel and stalked off down the hallway, expecting me to follow her. Of course I did. I had been working as Sasha's assistant for about a year now. She was a tough boss, but a fair one. Brilliant, yet patient. I was both intimidated by her and half in love with her, which was weird because I was straight.

At least I always thought I was.

There was just something about Sasha that made me wonder...I mean, if I'd go gay for anyone, it would definitely be my boss. She radiated a type of stern sex appeal that I'd found attractive ever since I'd started reading BDSM books in the privacy of my bedroom at night. Oddly enough, I'd never met a man whose sternness had the same effect on me.

I often wished that I had the courage to visit the BDSM club that the bosses supposedly frequented. That seemed like a good place to find myself a dom for the night. Or maybe a domme. I was just nervous that an actual dungeon would be too hard core for me. I was interested in spanking, maybe a little bondage, but I didn't want to be whipped or have someone pee on me or something.

When we got to Sasha's office she turned around and leaned against the corner of her large wooden desk. As usual, it was scrupulously organized. My face flushed as I imagined my boss laying me over the desk and spanking my ass red.

Tearing my gaze from the wood surface, I glanced at my boss. Sasha was tall and curvy, but not overly so. She was wearing a long black skirt with chunky high heeled boots and a dark red sweater that contrasted nicely with her pale white skin. Her dark black hair was in a perfect bob, the same as every day, and her dark red lipstick perfectly matched her sweater. She always looked incredibly put together, even after a twelve hour day at work.

"Close the door behind you, please Brandy."

I did as instructed, then walked towards the desk. I wondered how mad my boss was with me. She'd never really had a reason to reprimand me before. As usual, not a hint of emotion was showing on Sasha's beautiful face.

"If this is about my, um, eavesdropping, I'm --."

"Did you like what you heard?" she interrupted me.

"Um."

Sasha's voice dropped a few octaves. "Did you get off listening to Alina's punishment? If I were to slide my hand between those plump thighs of yours, would I discover wet panties?"

My eyes widened and my brain short-circuited as I imagined that very scenario. Meanwhile my traitorous pussy was sucking on air, desperate to be filled. Sasha stared at me with one eyebrow raised, clearly waiting for a response from me. The silence stretched before I finally answered.

"I did, um, find it interesting, yes," I stuttered. "I mean, it's not what I expected to overhear at the workplace."

The eyebrow raised more, her eyes growing more stern. "You found it interesting? Or arousing?"

"Arousing," I whispered, my face flushing with shame. God, I'd just admitted to my boss that I was some kind of spying pervert.

"Just as I thought. Your behavior today was not professional, Brandy," she scolded.

"Yes ma'am. I'm sorry."

Sasha's eyes widened slightly. I'd never called her ma'am before, and I wasn't sure why it had slipped out now.

"You know what I think, Brandy?"

Her voice was so soft I had to lean forward to hear her.

"No ma'am."

"I think that you're the kind of girl who longs to be taken in hand," she said thoughtfully. "You demonstrate a level of emotional immaturity that tells me that you've never been appropriately trained."

She crossed her arms underneath her breasts, the motion pushing them up like a gift. I consciously looked away. What was I doing ogling my boss's breasts?

"This isn't the first time I've caught you behaving unprofessionally. It's now clear to me that you want the same kind of punishment as Alina is getting. Crave it even. You need to be taught discipline and how to behave properly."

Sasha stared at me for a long moment, then added, "Take off your pants."

"What?" My voice rose several octaves.

"You will remove your pants please, and your underwear too," Sasha instructed, her voice as firm as I'd ever heard it. "Then bend over with your hands on the arms of that chair."

She pointed at one of the guest chairs across from her desk. It was a dark brown leather, with a high back and padded arms.

"Are you going to spank me?" I asked, my voice trembling. "Right here? Like Ruth did to Alina?"

"Yes, Brandy, I am going to spank you."

Her tone was calm and even, as if we were talking about preparing a report instead of me dropping my pants in my supervisor's office and being spanked like a naughty child.

"In fact, I'm going to spank you so hard you'll remember what you did wrong every time you try to sit down tomorrow...If you can sit down."

My mouth dropped open in shock even as a weird mixture of fear and excitement coursed through my body.

I'd fantasized about being spanked before – used it as a fantasy when I masturbated even -- but it had always been abstract. Hearing it happening in real life with Alina had made it real. Fueled my interest. Made me wet.

I'd heard some women found a spanking to be quite enjoyable. It had certainly sounded like my friend had been having a good time in there despite receiving what was clearly a hard spanking.

Yet somehow, I didn't think that Sasha was going to be focused on giving me pleasure. She was radiating cold anger. And God help me, but I found it incredibly attractive.

"Brandy!"

I jumped at her harsh growl of annoyance. Sasha jabbed a finger in the direction of the chair.

"Take off your pants and bend over. Don't make me ask you again. I promise it won't end well for you if I do."

Chapter Two: Getting More Than I Bargained For

I hustled to obey my supervisor's instructions. I knew that I could walk away – of course I could – it's not like she could fire me for not accepting a spanking. Could she? I didn't want to find out. I needed this job, and it paid very well.

Plus...I was curious. Dying to know what would happen. Would Sasha lose her famous composure? Would I?

I pulled off the black dress pants I'd worn to work, taking my underwear down with it, then folded everything neatly and slid onto the other guest chair. Keeping my back to her to hide my pussy, I leaned over the chair, gripping the arms with my hands, and looked over my shoulder.

Sasha was still leaning against the desk, watching my movements with a detached gaze.

"Do you want me like this?" I asked, my voice small.

I felt suddenly nervous. Baring myself, leaning over in a submissive position, it made this all real.

As usual, Sasha's face was inscrutable. She pushed away from the desk, walking closer to me. This close I could smell the subtle scent of her floral perfume.

"Face forward," she instructed as she placed a hand between my shoulder blades, pushing me down until I was in an "L" shape, my ass lifted up towards her.

My butt was not exactly small, and I wondered if Sasha was repulsed by the dimples of cellulite back there. I shivered as I felt her hand run over the bare skin. The woman had cold hands.

She explored my round globes with her fingers, then her hand slid down lower. I felt her push one finger between my pussy lips, and I wiggled in embarrassment, knowing exactly what she would find there. Sasha made a sound of disappointment.

"Just as I expected, you got off listening to your coworker being punished. You're completely wet, you dirty dirty girl."

A crack rang out, and it took about half a second to realize it was the sound of one of those cold hands slapping against my skin.

Thwack!

Thwack!

A stinging bloomed over my skin. Not terrible, but not pleasant either.

Sasha hit me twice in rapid succession, right on the same spot where the first two blows had fallen.

Thwack!

Thwack!

"Ow!"

The stinging turned to pain as my skin heated up. I shifted closer to the chair but was stopped by another sharp slap.

Thwack!

"Be still!" Sasha said firmly. "You will stay in place and take your punishment, or this will get much, much worse for you."

The juxtaposition between my position and her cold, calm voice was doing funny things to my insides.

Thwack!

Thwack!

Thwack!

Sasha switched to the other side and landed three hard spanks right in a row in the exact same place. The flesh of my ass vibrated from the assault, and I could feel heat rising where Sasha spanked me.

"You are a very bad girl, aren't you, Brandy?" Sasha asked.

Thwack!

"You will answer me when I ask you a question."

Thwack!

"Yes, I'm a bad girl," I said miserably as the spanking continued.

My punishment was harder and more painful than I expected, and it got worse with each strike of Sasha's palm.

Thwack!

Thwack!

"Tell me why you are being punished," she demanded.

"Because I spied on Alina and Ruth," I gasped.

Thwack!

Thwack!

"How would you like it if Alina or one of your other coworkers was trying to spy on you while you are being spanked like a naughty child?" my boss asked.

The chastisement added a level of humiliation that I wasn't expecting. And yet...the thought of someone catching us right now made me kind of hot. Hotter than I already was. More moisture flooded my core, dripping down my legs.

As if she knew what was happening, Sasha stopped spanking me and moved her hand between my legs again. Oh my God! Could she smell my arousal?

"Ah, I see. You quite like the idea of being humiliated in front of your coworkers, don't you?" Amusement laced her tone.

"No ma'am."

Thwack!

Thwack!

"Don't lie to me, Brandy!" she snapped, showing the tiniest break in her composure for the first time.

Suddenly Sasha shoved her finger in front of my face. "Clean your slutty juices off my finger you dirty girl."

Obediently I sucked her finger into my mouth, tasting myself on her skin.

"Perhaps next time I will make it happen. I would love to invite others into my office to watch your punishment," she said thoughtfully. "Or maybe I'll just do it in the conference room where everyone can see it at once."

I couldn't stop the moan that slipped past my lips.

"We'll save that for another time. This time, I want your sweet ass all to myself."

Thwack!

Thwack!

Thwack!

Thwack!

The spanking seemed to go on forever, as methodical as it was painful. Gradually, the pain emptied my mind, all my thoughts disappearing as I focused only on my aggrieved buttocks. They were throbbing with pain and heat. Somehow I kind of liked it.

Thwack!

Thwack!

I realized with a start that tears were dripping down my cheeks. I hadn't even realized that I was crying.

Thwack!

Thwack!

Sasha was completely silent as she went to town on my ass, and the silence made every spank reverberate through the room. I wondered if anyone was still working on the floor and if so, could they hear the sound of me being punished? The idea that someone was listening at the door the same way I'd done to Alina only a few minutes ago was both titillating and embarrassing.

Thwack!

Thwack!

Sasha was starting to slow down, longer pauses between each smack, and I breathed a sigh of relief that my punishment would be over soon. I wasn't sure how much more I could take before I became a blubbering mess, begging for relief. I resolved not to do that, knowing instinctively that it would disappoint my boss if I showed weakness.

I started to relax.

At least until she said, "Stay where you are. My palm is getting sore. I need to get my hairbrush."

I heard Sasha rustling around in her desk, then a large round brush appeared in front of my face. It was made out of polished wood, with a long handle and plastic bristles coming out of one side.

"I like to brush my hair at least a hundred strokes a day," Sasha said. "I have half a mind to give *you* a hundred strokes."

I gasped and she chuckled, but the sound was not at all amusement. It was painfully obvious that my boss was enjoying my discomfort.

"I'll give you only a dozen," she decided. "But if I catch you misbehaving again, I won't be as lenient with you next time Brandy, do you understand?"

When I didn't respond she fisted my long blonde hair right by the scalp, forcibly pulling my head backwards. Pain exploded through my scalp, but my pussy clenched at the same time. It was so confusing.

"I didn't hear you, Brandy!"

'Yes ma'am, I understand," I gasped.

The grip on my hair lightened, but she didn't let go. "Good girl."

Thwack!

The sting of the wooden brush against my ass was way more intense than the hand spanking had been, and I yelled out in pain, no longer worried about whether any of my coworkers would hear my cries. How was I going to take twelve of these?

Chapter Three: Not the Hairbrush!

I stood perfectly still, every muscle in my body frozen in place. Sasha's hand moved to the closest ass cheek, giving it a hard squeeze.

"If you clench it will only hurt worse, Brandy."

"Yes ma'am," I said, exhaling hard in an effort to relax.

Thwack!

"That was two, you have ten more to go."

Where the hand spanking had been steady, almost rhythmic, this was more erratic. I couldn't predict where or when the wooden brush would strike, or with what intensity.

Thwack!

A hard smack landed at the top of my ass, almost at my waist.

Thwack!

Another smack, this one right across my ass crack, catching a bit of both ass cheeks.

Thwack!

This one hit me right where my butt connected to my thighs, and it hurt harder than anything I'd ever experienced. Possibly ever.

"Fuck!" I yelled, tears falling down my face. "That really hurts!"

"It's supposed to hurt," Sasha said calmly as she caught the meaty part of my left ass cheek with the wooden end of the brush. "It's a punishment, not a love tap. You're lucky I'm not using a belt."

Thwack!

Thwack!

I was sobbing now, my breath coming in big gulps, a steady stream of tears falling from my eyes.

Thwack!

Thwack!

I lost count as the brush continued to rain down on my skin. All of my attention was focused on the movements behind me, trying to anticipate where it would strike me next.

My ass was burning, as if it were on fire. My hands twitched, desperate to rub my aggrieved flesh. It felt like Sasha had flayed the skin right off my ass cheeks.

As if reading my thoughts, Sasha remarked, "Your ass is cherry red."

Her voice was pure satisfaction.

Thwack!

Sasha paused, and the only sound in the room was our breathing.

"That was twelve," Sasha finally said. "Have you learned your lesson, Brandy?"

"Yes ma'am," I sniffed.

She stepped away, but I didn't dare move. The air was cool over my naked ass, relieving some of the stinging. I waited breathlessly for whatever was going to happen next.

"Stand up."

I winced as I moved to standing, the movement making my glutes flex.

"Turn around."

I followed her instructions, but I was too embarrassed to meet Sasha's eyes.

"Well, what a pretty pussy you have." Sasha's voice was softer than I'd ever heard it, almost sweet.

I silently thanked the universe that I'd just gotten a wax the other day. This experience was mortifying enough without having bad grooming in the mix.

Sasha stepped forward and pulled my shirt over my head, leaving me standing there in nothing but a bra. I shivered as a burst of air from the air conditioner brushed my skin.

I wasn't sure what was happening now, but when my boss reached between my breasts to release the front clasp of my bra, I shimmied the garment down off my shoulders without a word.

Sasha walked around me in a slow circle, making me acutely aware that I was buck naked, and she was still fully clothed. She stepped up behind me until my back was pressed against her front, the soft fabric of her skirt sliding against my aching ass cheeks.

"You took your spanking well," she said in a voice that was almost detached. "Much better than I expected. I thought for sure you'd break when I brought out the hairbrush. Lift your arms please."

Without hesitation, I brought my arms out into a T. I felt Sasha's arms slide around my naked torso, one hand settling on each of my breasts. She cupped my tits in her hands, as if testing their weight, then gave them each a firm squeeze. My hips jerked in reaction, seeking pressure.

"Place your hands on top of your head," she whispered into my ear. "If you leave them there, you will get a reward. If you move them, I will punish you more instead."

I shivered but followed her instructions, threading my fingers together and placing them on top of my head. Sasha bit my earlobe, hard enough that I gasped.

"Good girl."

She began kneading my breasts roughly, paying special attention to the nipples. I was already aroused, but the fondling of my sensitive breasts only ratcheted up my excitement. I arched my back, pressing myself into her hands while my hips jerked back and forth greedily.

Sasha mimicked my movements, grinding herself against my ass before lowering her hands to my hips.

"Widen your legs."

I stepped out a bit and she shifted her right hand between my lower lips, one finger moving into my weeping channel. In this position, I was trapped against her body, surrounded by her arms. Squeezing me even closer to her, Sasha began fucking me with her finger while her other hand found my clit.

I gasped. Without a word, Sasha rubbed her thumb against my swollen bud, pressing it against my pelvic bone.

My hands slid to my forehead, but I quickly snapped them back up to the top of my head to stay in position. I was completely under Sasha's control, mindless with pleasure. I heard myself making soft whining sounds as my orgasm neared.

"You can't come yet," Sasha ordered.

I groaned in frustration. She removed her hands from my pussy, gripping my waist with one hand as she gave me several hard slaps right over my aching clit with the other.

The sharp slaps over my clit had me digging the tips of my fingers into the top of my head, trying to obey Sasha's order not to come. I was close, so close, and hanging on by the thinnest thread.

"Behave, or I won't let you come at all."

"Yes ma'am," I said softly, heaving a sigh of relief when her hands returned to my slick core, stroking me in earnest.

Sasha nipped along the top of my shoulder with her teeth as she continued to fuck me with her hands. My entire body was vibrating with arousal, making me pant for breath.

"Please ma'am, please," I gasped, unable to stay silent any longer. "I need to come so bad. Please!"

"I love the sound of you begging," she whispered. "You may come now."

Sharp teeth sunk into the flesh of my shoulder, hard enough to bruise, and I shrieked as the strongest orgasm that I'd ever experienced in my life raced through my body.

Sasha's arms tightened against me as I thrashed in her arms, but somehow I kept my hands on top of my head. My knees started to buckle, and Sasha released me as I sank to the floor. I landed on my knees, then flopped onto the ground like a fish as I shuddered through the aftershocks. The tremors were just fading when I heard Sasha's voice behind me.

"Roll over," she ordered.

As I flipped onto my back, I realized that she'd removed her skirt and panties. I eyed her neatly trimmed pussy greedily, desperate for a taste. As if she could read my mind, Sasha sank to her knees.

She crawled up my body until she was sitting on my chest, knees on either side of my shoulders. I could feel the moistness of her cunt against my bare sternum.

"Thank me for your punishment."

"Thank you ma'am," I whispered, too spent from my orgasm to feel any embarrassment at yet another humiliation. "Thank you for punishing me."

She nodded, a hint of a smile playing at her red, red lips. I wondered what it would take for her to give me a full smile.

"Now that you've gotten a reward, I need one as well. It's time for you to please the boss."

Chapter Four: Riding My Face

S asha moved forward on her knees until her core was lined up with my face. I eyed her curiously. I'd never been this up close and personal with the female anatomy before, other than looking at myself in the mirror, and I was surprised how pretty this particular area was.

As I gazed up at Sasha's pink pussy, noticing how slick she was, my mouth watered. Her lower lips glistened with arousal. Clearly she'd gotten off on what had just happened as much as I did. She lowered herself down until her cunt hovered just above my face.

"You will make me come now," she ordered. "Use your tongue."

If I'd wanted to protest, it was too late because the next thing I knew, she was literally sitting on my face. Tentatively I opened my mouth and stuck out my tongue, sliding it between her pussy lips.

I'd never tasted a woman's arousal other than hints of my own when I'd kissed a partner after they'd gone down on me. But as I lapped up Sasha's cream, I found I liked it. It tasted way better than any boyfriend's cum that I'd tried, a little bit sweeter and creamier somehow.

Even though I was pleasuring her, my boss was still in control. The press of her inner thighs against my ears muffled most of the sound in the room. Her hands reached back to pin my shoulders to the floor. I liked the feeling of being dominated by Sasha, being trapped under her weight.

I mean, I could push her off, of course I could, but I didn't want to. I was enjoying this too much.

Even though I'd just had a powerful orgasm, I was getting aroused from the simple act of flattening my tongue and sliding it through Sasha's folds. I experimented with pressure and speed, quickly learning what she liked.

When Sasha was actively moving her pussy against my face, I changed tactics. Circling the tip of my tongue around her entrance, I slowly slid it inside her tight channel. Sasha moaned above me.

"Yes, my pet. Fuck me with your tongue."

I started pumping in and out of her in earnest, then acting on instinct – or at least based on what worked for my own body -- I slid my hand between us and explored her folds until I found the tight bud of her clit. Placing my pointer finger on one side and my middle finger on the other, I moved along the edge of her swollen bundle of nerves, back and forth, back and forth, then I pressed my fingers together to give her clit a little pinch.

Sasha jumped as if she had been electrified.

"Do it again," she ordered with a moan. "But with more pressure."

When I complied, giving her clit a harder pinch this time, Sasha made a keening sound. She fell forward until her hands hit the floor, bracing herself as she ground her body against my face.

I continued fucking her with my tongue and pinching and releasing her clit until she finally came undone over me. Moisture flooded my tongue, and I lapped it up as fast as I could while Sasha quivered and moaned with the force of her orgasm.

I'd never seen my boss be anything but completely in control, and knowing that I'd done this to her, that I had pleasured her enough that she'd lost control, it was the best feeling in the world.

Releasing her clit, I continued to lick her as she came down from her orgasm, then used my tongue to lap up the rest of the cream that had flooded her pussy.

When she finally stopped trembling, Sasha rolled off my face, laying on the floor to one side of me. Her breath was coming in long pants and when I looked up, her face was softer than I'd ever seen it, her eyes closed, and a satisfied smile lifting the corners of her lips.

I glanced down and realized that she was still wearing her blouse, still fully dressed from the waist up. It thrilled me to know that she'd wanted me so badly she hadn't taken the time to do more than bare her bottom half.

I wondered idly if I'd get to see her tits next time. I had a feeling that they were fantastic.

I stared up at the ceiling, my mind racing as I tried to process everything that had happened. My face was glistening with moisture and when I licked my lips, I could still taste Sasha there.

After a few moments of silence, she pushed herself to sitting, and I did the same, oddly unconcerned about my nakedness. Sasha met my eyes, her gaze speculative.

"Have you gone down on a woman before, Brandy?" she asked curiously.

"No ma'am, you're the first."

Something flared in her eyes. It looked almost...possessive.

"Well, I have to tell you that you're quite good at it. A natural."

I felt unaccountably pleased at her praise, pleased that I'd brought her as much pleasure as she'd brought me.

"I might have to keep you late after work more often," she continued. "That is, if you can keep yourself from eavesdropping on your coworkers."

I gave her a saucy smile.

"Will you spank me again if I do?"

One corner of her mouth quirked up, like she was trying to decide whether to smile or maintain her stern appearance.

"Definitely."

"We'll have to do this again some time I guess."

Giving her a coy smile, I realized that I was somehow flirt-ing with my boss, and more amazingly, she was kind of – almost – flirting back.

"Are you dating anyone, Brandy?"

My eyes flew to hers. Was she thinking what I was?

"No, I'm not dating anyone right now."

Sasha nodded, looking pleased. "You are now."

"Are you saying what I think you're saying?" I asked.

For the first time since I'd met her, Sasha looked the tiniest bit uncertain.

"The truth is, Brandy, that I've been...attracted to you for a while. But I thought you were straight, so I never acted on it."

"I am," I responded. "Or at least I was. I've never been attracted to a woman before. Until now."

"I need to be clear, if we are together, I will be in charge, at all times. I don't tolerate disobedience in my personal life any more than I do at the office."

"I understand."

She raised one eyebrow, her face looking stern again. I pressed my thighs together as my greedy pussy flooded with moisture again.

"Yes ma'am," I amended. "I understand."

"Good girl. Now get dressed so I can take you home with me. I've got a special playroom there I'd like you to see."

***

If you liked this book, please leave me a rating or review.

Be sure follow Josie Bale to be the first to hear about new releases, check it out at https://www.amazon.com/author/josiebale

SPECIAL PREVIEW: THE RELUCTANT BRIDE'S FIRST SPANKING BY JOSIE BALE

A SPANKING THERAPY CLINIC ADVENTURE

"Are we ever going to get married Rebecca?"

Jacob's forceful words burst out suddenly in the silent room, fast and loud, making me jump. I looked up from my e-reader with a frown.

"What?" I asked. "Where is this coming from?"

Jacob moved closer to me on the couch, reaching to take my hand. His touch was familiar and comforting. He stared at me intently until I looked up and met his deep blue eyes.

"I don't understand what the problem is, Rebecca," he said earnestly. "I asked you to marry me two years ago, and you keep refusing to set a date. We've been together five years now. Don't you love me anymore?"

I suppressed a sigh. "Yes, of course I do Jacob, it's, just –"

"What?" he asked impatiently, shaking his head. A lock of his thick blonde hair fell over his forehead with the motion, giving him a boyish appearance that belied his 35 years.

I studied him for a long moment, choosing my words carefully. "I don't feel ready yet," I finally answered lamely. "I need more time."

Jacob's handsome face pinched with frustration. "More time? It's been five years!" he pointed out. "What's holding you back? We have a good thing, right? We love each other. We're compatible. I just don't get it."

I shook my head miserably and looked at my fingers twisting in my lap. "I'm sorry Jacob," I whispered. "I do love you, you know I do, but I'm just not ready. Not yet."

"When will you be ready Rebecca?" he asked. "Will you ever be ready? Or am I supposed to wait forever?"

I shook my head, my eyes filling with tears. When I didn't say anything more, he got up off the couch and stalked out of the room without another word, leaving me alone with my thoughts.

I couldn't blame him for being angry, I had been putting him off for a long time. The truth was, I had a nagging sense of dissatisfaction with our relationship. I truly loved Jacob, but something was missing. I couldn't quite put my finger on it, so I had no idea how to discuss it with him.

My girlfriends all told me I was crazy to not have locked him down already. Jacob was the perfect man: attentive, generous, supportive, and kind. He had a good job, worked out, ate healthy, didn't drink excessively or smoke or do drugs. He treated me like a princess.

And not that this was a deal breaker or anything, but he was quite good looking: about six feet tall with wide shoulders, washboard abs, brilliant blue eyes, and a strong chin with a dimple in the center. Honestly, he could have been a model.

We had a lot of fun together and we were quite compatible. The only negative really was that our love making was…. just fine. Vanilla. Kind of bland. It was nothing to write home about. Jacob was a missionary man, if you know what I mean. He mostly gravitated to that one position, resisting my efforts to try something else. And we rarely had sex outside of the bed. Shower sex was a special treat in our world.

Don't get me wrong, Jacob almost always got me off, he was really considerate that way. He was a master of eating pussy, quite talented in that department. But I longed for some passion, some excitement, something less predictable.

Sometimes when I was home alone, I would burrow under the covers with my vibrator and fantasize about a different kind of lover: someone who would push me up against a wall, shove aside my panties and really fuck me, hard and rough, like he couldn't wait another moment to be inside me. Someone who would take me from behind while slapping my ass. Someone who would talk dirty and pinch my nipples.

It was ridiculous really. Here I was, a dyed-in-the-wool feminist engaged to an enlightened man who treated me like an equal and I longed for someone more alpha. Just in the bedroom, mind you. I did not want to be bossed around in real life, but a little domination in the bedroom? That's what got me off in my private moments. But there was no way I could tell Jacob that.

Later that night I lay awake in the bed, listening to Jacob snoring softly, and tried to convince myself to set a date for the wedding. I told myself I should either marry him or break up with him. But I couldn't do either. Was this all there was?

The next day I woke up in a funk. I had a bad feeling that Jacob was nearing the end of his patience and even though I wasn't ready to marry him, I didn't want to lose him either. I sat in the coffee shop near my office, brooding as I sipped my chai latte and thumbed through our city's alternative weekly. Suddenly an ad seemed to jump off the page.

"Do you need to be punished? Do you have emotional blocks preventing you from living your best life? Our experienced Spanking Therapists can help set you straight. Call today."

My heart was pounding as I read and re-read that ad. Did I dare? I had never even heard of spanking therapy, but

I couldn't deny that the thought of being spanked by a stranger was strangely titillating. And I couldn't get past the thought that this might be exactly what I needed to get past whatever was bothering me and help me to make up my mind about my relationship with Jacob. Maybe if I just tried it once I could get it out of my system and settle down with Jacob.

Before I could change my mind, I locked myself into the single stall restroom and made the call. A professional sounding woman picked up and explained how the process worked.

"I'll send you a questionnaire via email to fill out and return to us. You might find it a bit intrusive but it's really necessary for us to design the best therapeutic experience for you so please answer honestly," the woman explained. "Once we receive the questionnaire and your deposit, I will contact you to schedule your first appointment."

"How many appointments does it usually take?" I asked timidly, feeling a little over my head.

"It depends on the person," the lady answered. "Some people come once and experience a level of catharsis that lets them move on. Others prefer to come in regularly, kind of like maintenance. It'll be up to you and the therapist to figure out a treatment plan that works best for you and your particular issues."

Before I could change my mind, I went back to my table in the coffee shop and filled out the extensive questionnaire in my e-mail, sending it back with a $250 deposit. My hands shook as I pressed "send". Excitement and dread warred for my attention. Would I have the guts to actually do this? Would it help?

Within an hour I received an email back offering me an appointment for the following day. Suddenly I felt resolved to check it out. Spanking therapy....it was worth a try, right?

For more of the story, check out "The Reluctant Bride's First Spanking" by Josie Bale, part of the "Spanking Therapy Series" available now at https://www.amazon.com/dp/B0CY3YRQ4V

OTHER BOOKS BY JOSIE BALE

Follow Josie Bale to receive email updates for all new releases. For more information visit https://mailchi.mp/5031b4165265/josie-newsletter-sign-up

The Sapphic Submission Series

Punished By the Boss

Pleasing the Boss

Tied Up By the Boss

Dominated By the Boss

The Divorce Recovery Series

Spanking Justice: A Middle-Aged Divorcee's First Spanking

A Punishing Workout: Spanked by the Trainer

A Disciplined Budget: Spanked by the Accountant

The Spanking Therapy Series

The Reluctant Bride's First Spanking

The Reluctant Bride Gets Caught

The Billionaire Gets Punished

The Curvy Reporter Gets Punished

Unlikely Doms Series

Alpha in a Sweater Vest

Alpha Plumber

Hotel Spanking

Alpha Student

Alpha Yogi

The Punishing Holidays Series

Turkey and a Spanking

Shopping and a Spanking

Presents and a Spanking

Be sure to follow Josie's author page on your favorite retailer!

ABOUT JOSIE BALE

J osie Bale loves nothing more than to feel the sting of a palm on her backside. Or a brush. Or a strap. She's not picky, as long as she's getting what she wants.

Her stories feature the lighter side of BDSM including spanking, bondage, and power play. Be sure to follow Josie on your favorite retailer and sign up for her newsletter to be the first to hear about new releases, giveaways, and special sales. For more information visit https://mailchi .mp/5031b4165265/josie-newsletter-sign-up.

Printed in Great Britain
by Amazon